INK AND FABLE

BookSquirrel Publications

Ink and Fable

Book *Squirrel* Publication

Regd. Under MSME Act.

"INK AND FABLE"

By: author name/s

ISBN:978-93-89557-38-1

Language: English

1ˢᵗ Edition

Formatting: Muskan Shah

Cover: Mr_Ash

Ink and Fable

<u>DISCLAIMER</u>

This anthology is a fiction. The compiler has tried her best to edit and curate the content of the co-authors and made it plagiarism free.

All the write ups in this book are unique.

In case of any plagiarism detected, neither the compiler nor the publishers are responsible. Co-authors will be solely responsible for their own content.

<u>ACKNOWLEDGEMENT</u>

The making of this anthology would not have been possible without the co-authors. A gratitude towards all who have worked hard and have made effort for this book to be a success.

I am thankful to BookSquirrel Publication, without whom this project would not be possible.

Above all, the hearty thanks to my parents and friends for supporting me throughout this project. Lastly, I am thankful to the almighty for giving me this opportunity and strength to complete it successfully.

COMPILER

This is Aditi Gupta from Haridwar, Uttarakhand. She is currently pursuing degree in biotechnology from Dehradun, Uttarakhand. She aspires to be an IAS officer. She is a passionate rifle shooter and a traveller. She loves to be lost while writing.

REMINISCENCE OF PAST

It's been a year now,

I don't bother you

But, u know what love

The rain bothers me a lot

It always made me feel

Like a part of me is apart now

From a year,

I am trying to convince me

To forget you

But I failed

and deep inside I love to be failed in it

Your memories are like drugs to me now

I want to get rid of it, but don't know how

Yes, I agree

Yes, I agree

That I love you

But it's like stabbing myself

Ink and Fable

My heart still says

I am all yours forever

But, that reality

That reality hit the heart hard

Broken pieces are shattered badly

Come love, gather them...

-Aditi Gupta

Dear Readers, these tales belong to you…

FLYING BIRD

Like a bird I want to fly..

Above the clouds, high and high

The desire within is simply simple,

Make love and kiss the sky

Like a bird I don't care of the ground below,

Where I'll lose myself

Challenges!! I want to dare the adventures of life,

Which I'll choose myself..

Before I die, I need to fly

The purpose of life, Is still a "Why"

My life has become, A fake bonsai!!

The feathers of dreams, Is on standby!!

The sky is happy, I don't want to cry!!

Now the time, For me to reply!!

I'm going over clouds, to make myself satisfy

Then only I'll have, the sweetest goodbye!!

-Abhinandan Srivastava

PRICE

What we see isn't reality!!

What we can't isn't a lie!!

The price of both is the worth unidentified!!

To find the worth, is still a "Why"!!

The price of breath is always the same.. right!!

So what's the difference between you and I?

The memories we cherish, and the few we forget!!

Is the price of time!!

The poems I wrote !!

And the thoughts I collect!!

Is the price of rhyme!!

The price of smile, The price of laughter..

The price of eyes, And their leaking water

The price of family, And the love they give

The price of death, Is the price we live..

-Abhinandan Srivastava

FRIENDS AND TRUTH

I crave for friends

Why are friends so rare?

Yet one is enough,

Through faith, love and care.

.

I look for truth

I try and I grope

How truth may be found?

I don't know..

It bears no fruit

Friends are real, yet unreal

Like envelops, their inside sealed

No one wants to open his own

So everyone has himself veiled.

Truth seems near, yet so far

You can't find it in the bar

Nor can you dig it up, from the ground

May be you will find it by chance..

-Abu Md Zakaria

QUOTES:-

Your negative feedback always make you more stable.

-Abu Md Zakaria

QUOTES:-

I am selfish, impatient and a little insecure. I make mistakes, I am out of control and at times hard to handle. But if you cannot handle me at my worst, then you sure as hell don't deserve me at my best.

-Adityan Dravid

Love is totally nonsensical. But we have to keep doing it or else we are lost and love is dead, and humanity should just pack it in. because love is the best thing we do.

-Adityan Dravid

You can make more friends in two months by showing interest in other people than you can in two years, by trying to get other people interested in you.

-Adityan Dravid

CLOSEST STRANGER

It's 3AM, you are all alone thinking about your messed up life, complicated relationships, heart breaks fake friends. Whom you need now? A stranger…. A person who is totally strange to you, a person who doesn't even know a single thing about you. This person is a plain canvas… u can share everything with them without any fear of getting jugged by them. They can not have you. They don't know about your weaknesses and strengths. They might come out to be the closest stranger you have ever met. Sometimes all you need is — A stranger because you have already ditched by your close ones

-Ahtesham

RELATIONSHIP RULES

Regarding relationships, I have just one rule; give me truth, however cold or cruel or hard it is to hear. I would prefer to have my heart bled and broken if it means I can then move on, then waste a single moment of my time being fooled by a lie intended to preserve my feelings.

-Ahtesham

BEST FRIEND

"Best friend" is not just a word.

A best friend is someone who is there for you, no matter what. Through thick and thin, I can label anyone as a friend.

But a best friend?

That's something that needs to be earned. A best friend knows me sometimes more than I know myself. Best friend share tears and laughs. You can trust them with anything and everything. I have a bunch of friends, but only a few that I can count on completely.

-Ahtesham

REFLECTION

I saw the reflection walking out of the mirror. Every bit of it looked like me than the blood stains and dirt. The room was filled with the smell of rotten flesh and I stood still, not moving a limb. Closer it was, the darker I felt. With the time I realised I was trapped inside the mirror and I could see my reflection standing outside, clean like I was. But now I feel cold, dirty and drenched inside the mirror

-Aiswarya Bose

HOW I WAS SAVED

Writing saved me from this world. I would have been long gone, leaving a framed photograph decorated with lights or flowers garlands on the wall and a little pain in few caring hearts, if not I figured out that I can make my world better, writing unreal and believing it's real.

A life full of worry and hate written as a life full of love and care until get used to the world.

-Aiswarya Bose

DOORS AND DEMONS

I have this problem with open and closed doors. At mornings, when there is plenty of light outside, I am too scared to close the doors, it feels like a demon inside my house will conquer me if I do. And at night I am too scared to leave the doors open, because it feels like something will pull me into the darkness if I do.

-Aiswarya Bose

DREAMS

Last night, I saw you

You kissed my forehead and said.

"Honey, I'm here now"

I couldn't believe my eyes.

I touched your hand

Which was as cold as ice.

I don't know why, but I believed you.

Lying side by side,

We laughed over jokes.

We cried over memories, I looked into your eyes,

Which were shining brighter than any gem could ever.

I realized how much I missed you all these years.

Suddenly, you said, "I've got to go",

"No" , I pleaded.

You promised me to come again but I was too reluctant to let you
go..

Ink and Fable

At last, you said,

"Honey, it isn't real"

My world shattered.

I opened my eyes and witnessed the snowfall from the window.

Your gravestone was covered in snow.

I cried for you,

For all of our beautiful memories,

For all the dreams that we had together,

For all those painful nights when we missed each other,

Indeed that wasn't real,

But dear, I promise you that we would meet again,

Every night

In my dreams…

-Ankita Saloni

MY PARENTS

That was the time when you both held my hand,

I was very new on this land.

Time was like handful of sand,

You both gave me strength to stand.

When I would cry and be up all night,

You would sit and ignore your sleep all night.

You both are sunlight of my day,

You both are moonlight of my dark pathway.

You both are the words inside my song,

If you are with me I can never be wrong.

You are the ones who cares for me,

You are the eyes that help me see.

My eyes will search only for you wherever I go,

You are the greatest friend I know

You are both special in every way,

Encouraging me more and more every passing day.

You are the most precious gift that life grants,

You are my love, my life, my parents…

-Annu

ALWAYS YOURS

I may not be perfect as such,

I may not be deserving as much,

I don't wander in temples,

I don't tell when my soul trembles,

I may not give you friendly looks,

I may not look for solutions in holy book,

I may pretend like a demon,

I may be the one who ignores,

But it's ok..

I will still be always yours…

-Annu

INDIAN BEAUTY

In ripped jeans, kurti and bindi with open hair,

Comes my Indian beauty down from the stairs,

She is embodiment of same elegance and passion,

She walks like soothing breeze but,

She is also the storm that shows no compassion.

What has changed in her, you ask

She understood protecting her is not her man's task,

She is not just breathing but living now,

She has her own voice which is clear and loud,

With pride, head high

She walks on every floor,

She doesn't hides behind the doors,

Her wedding rings are a chain no more,

These are just options for her to explore…

-Annu Priya

UNSOLICITED ONE

I wonder what makes it a weed, a sieve

But then it wasn't useful to you

So it must be futile

I wonder why you defy the evil

What makes it so sure you aren't the devil

Maybe it's the white you wear

Maybe being camouflaged in the dark is your biggest fear…

Oh, I know you but we aren't so same,

I wear my black, I was never ashamed

I must know you, I was the grass you defamed

What was my fault, it's hard to remember

Yes, I was the plant that couldn't be tamed…

-Annu Priya

QUOTES:-

It's true crying will make your heart light but it's also true that choking your tears will make you a stronger person..

-Anshu Kumar Choudhary

Life won't give you everything you ask for but that doesn't mean you should stop trying to achieve it.

Fear from worthless not failure.

-Anshu Kumar Choudhary

It's alright if your quotes don't inspire anyone, may be your success would inspire more rather than quoting.

WORK FOR SUCCESS NOT QUOTES.

-Anshu Kumar Choudhary

QUOTES:-

You know what is the most romantic thing for me?

Hug?

Kiss?

"No"

When I get mad at you and you calm me by buying books and read poetries to me..

-Bhojani Ayesha Asif

She was angry at him, he bought 'Diwan-e-ghalib' for her and some cds of ghazalas,

Her anger melted,

He knows how to handle mood swings of his fluffy panda.

-Bhojani Ayesha Asif

After a fight,

When they were having dinner,

He played her favourite show and she served his favourite meal,

In anger too…

Care always remains constant..

-Bhojani Ayesha Asif

THE REAL YOU

You are so real that,

Imagination of most wonderful appearance becomes disappeared,

You are so real that memories of imagining you are faded,

You are so real that chanting of devotees is lagging behind,

You are so real that I become feared hallucinating you,

You are so real that incarnation of lord will be dissolved with the time,

You are so real that my whole is mendacious to me,

You belong to me only as most realistic substance.

-Chandra Ghosh

LET ME WRITE

As long as I'm writing, I am growing more to explore my thoughts

The thoughts that is unspoken,

Hidden in unconscious mind.

As long as I'm writing, I am floating beyond the imagination

The imagination which cannot be connected with harsh reality .

As long as I'm writing, I am breaking my delighted heart

A heart is creating that is broken, dilapidated.

-Chandra Ghosh

FRAGRANCE

It was not the appearance to whom I chased, it was only the fragrance of yours which bound me to your fantasy world and to get trapped in it. It was something different and very unusual that your fragrance just fades every others near to it but now it has been changed gradually with time.

-Deep Roy

SCIENTIFIC LOVE

I had exerted a force of 7newton on a body. Due to some foreign particles now it has become 700newton and I think that the body will recognize Newton's third law of motion and will forward that 700newton to 7000newton and so on…

-Deep Roy

Back in time

It was shivering cold even in the month of August back in time, the rain would make us to bring out blanket in the late summer back in time, preparation of fire woods would start before the winter back in time, all the people were known to us back in time. Forest were more dense back in time even the water bodies were beautiful as it was more pure back in time, there was more love of affection for everyone back in time but all changed with time, the sad part of the human evolution…

It was much better BACK IN TIME…

-Deep Roy

BLOOD SHOT EYES

31

Wander the city of Kashi. Take a break from your plastic life. You can see death doing window shopping. Blood shots eyes of sages who has seen demons of hell. Darkness they live, made home. They dwell with ghost and goblins. Souls of souls they have seen departed fron one room to another. And here we are writing and scribbling about some nonsense. First time we cried when we took inhalation and we are borne in to his mad world living a timetable. I say, all you boys and girls out there crush it, dump it in to the dustbin and live a life. Don't forget ever that we are all the children of the grave.

-Deepak Ninkileri

DARK IMPULSION

They live in your room, Don't you see them? They come next to you all pull your blankets when you are lost in some illusion of dream. Night crawlers they are coming back. Sing your prayers as it won't be answered as they come in peace and protection. Angel's of darkness my friends. They don't tell you some Bollywood life stories which will make you so emotional. they destroys you so that next day when you wake up, you are reborn. Make your bed a grave. We are all the children of the grave, that's the ultimate truth. You want to get lost in so called crazy breed like society? You want to live a plastic life? Ask yourself...

-Deepak Ninkileri

DESIDERIUM

I feel impotent,

My dreams are shattered,

Dreams! I painted my childhood days,

Anticipated to have accomplished,

Turned to be a fiasco now.

Consenting my fate and moving on,

With a heavy heart,

Pushing each second in fathomless distress,

Why me? Only me!

Where I feel like an artist,

Whose painting water split,

wrecked and Desolated!!

-Devika Radhakrishnan

ENIGMA

Somewhere profoundly I,

Ascertain a hunch of vacuity,

Unable to apprehend,

the reason causing.

Exasperating every now and then,

clutched on to me like,

There's no plan to leave.

Constantly probing,

Unable to resolve.

Where am I resolve.

Where am I wrong?

Fabricating hiatus everywhere!

Where I'm impotent to do anything..

-Devika Radhakrishnan

MY MATE

God gifted you as a surprise,

Having you is like a golden prize.

You hold me like a feather,

Make me feel loved in every weather.

One, who is needed to lean on in devil's own luck,

Can't go to else, just got stuck.

People says, it's hard to find a loyal mate-

But surely divinity wrote for me a golden fate.

In my counterfeit grin you found that bewailing silence-

Treats me like a chuffed kid by confronting to my love, grace and violence.

It must not be easy to became a part of this frenzied life

And bearing my words which feels like a lacerating knife.

Abstemious personality of yours may not attracts assemblage,

But it makes to lock up my hands with your until I'll be free from almighty given life's cage.

-Disha Sharma

QUOTES:-

Stars bloom, night shines- heart starts to fall in love but carefully, almighty's nature is to catechize you on every step to bless you with bestowal.

-Disha Sharma

PUBG LIFE

PUBG is not just a game

Make new friends in a struggle,

New way of life,

New way of battle,

There will be lots of enemy like a society,

Who wants you to get out of your destination,

And lost your medals,

So fight with all your enemy

To move forward and get a successful life.

-G Bala Gomathi

SOMEWHERE INSIDE YOU

You are my only aspiration to get me back,

You are the biggest dream I chased for,

You are the top secret that never revealed,

You are the only robber to steal my heart,

Trust me! I will always be there for you,

Love me you are my everything I meant to be,

Be mine forever my love!!

-G Bala Gomathi

QUOTES:-

If you have any problem with anyone, say it to the one with whom you have problem, if you tell it to any other person then that third person will make it more confusing.

-Harsh Karnwal

If something wrong is going on in your life don't say anything to anyone, don't be depressed. Wait fir the right time everything will be alright.

-Harsh Karnwal

Friendship is the only relationship in which we don't think about self-respect. But if you feel ignored in the friendship then move on you are born for that friendship.

-Harsh Karnwal

STAR-GAZING

As the world sleeps,

I lay on the fields leaving my struggles below,

Wondering how high they are;

They leave me in awe.

Silently, from behind the clouds,

The moon shines as I lay there losing track of my time.

-Karthik

ROAD TRIP

Breathing in fresh air,

Feeling the wind through my hair,

Venturing into the unknown each second,

The beauty of road trip,

I reckon avoiding potholes and paying tolls,

Life to me is not a beach but a road trip

-Karthik

YOU

Eyes speak more than words will ever do

There's no one in this world I love, as much as I love you

Life will pass by but the happiest hours of mine will be when I am
with you

Nothing is forever except my memories and in those memories,
forever, there will be you.

-Karthik

QUOTES:-

Excuses of situations have always been lame to me!

Do you know why?

Because if situation is not making me to achieve it, I will add all my energy to mold it,

And in the end I would make that mine..

This is why I call myself insane!

-Lavi Chaudhry

Become so precious that people crave for your single appearance.

-Lavi Chaudhry

There is only one criteria to get success in the life and in my language it is called 'Endless Insanity'.

-Lavi Chaudhry

ILLUSION OF HAPPINESS

Sure, she laughs, she sings-

Her smile brightens up the room

But you'd never know that-

Her days are dark and gloom.

She feels the constant fear and pain,

But her swollen eyes still glow-

Though every tear fall like rain.

Her calm face will never let you know-

That her life is an ongoing sin,

Where the flame of burning comes from within.

She seems a girl who is full of life,

Where only happiness lies-

But you'd never know that every night oft she dies!

She is playing a happy role,

Where happiness is the only dramatic part-

While hiding the truth, the thorns of life is just breaking her heart.

The girl you see is just a happy girl in disguise,

And you'd never know the truth,

Because it's hard to read her eyes!

-Mahmoda Sultana (Mahi)

FRIENDSHIP

We make so many friends,

Some become dearest,

Some become special,

Some go abroad,

Some left us,

Some ignored us,

We ignored some

Some are in contact,

Some are not in contact,

Some don't contact because of their ego,

We don't contact some because of our ego,

Whatever they were,

We still remember, love, miss, care for them!

Because of their part they play to make memories.

That is FRIENDSHIP!!

-Mohamed Asif

QUOTES:-

You can't make everyone think as deeply as you do. That's your tragedy. Because you understand them, they cannot understand you!

-Mohamed Asif

Wise one get fooled when he think himself as wise!

-Mohamed Asif

QUOTES:-

Sky sure is blue, suffering a flu without the visible creatures flying through but with those awesome invisible gestures causing through and it spreads rumours through speaking 90's made are the only true behind it's dim light filled with gust of dust.

-Mohnish

From the time I was nine till the calendar turned 2k19, sadness never left my door knocked.

-Mohnish

My nerve shrinks hard every second, me being alive paying the guilt the price of pain, I never deserve in my name.

-Mohnish

CONFESSION OF LOVE

Every night I see a dream, Now I want to make you my dream. I gave you my heart at first sight, I think I should make you my life now.

The journey to meet you and see you till the last time is beautiful, I want to keep going like this by holding your hand.

Most say that you are my life, I want to see my face in your beautiful eyes. Whenever the words have come out of my lips, They have the name of you. Although, love is a beautiful feeling, I want to live this feeling with you.

This is all I have to say to you, I have to be in your eyes forever. Have a heartbeat with your heart.

If you say yes, I want to hold myself in your arms.

Just hold one hand and make you mine, With other hand I will make a paradise for you. I love you with my heart and always will. What has happened so far, I am doing everything for you, Because life has to be spent with you. I love you and I want to feel the magic which people called love

-Morgan Malla

LOVE STORY

You still want me to say,

I am special for you But where is a way, you have to prove yourself right and wrong to me, I am waiting for you every evening, waiting for you every night, these days many births take place, till the evening falls under your love, they also fall apart. And my only wish is that you talk to me about doing something like this from the sky, pray every moon again for you. Many stories are incomplete, many solicitation are incomplete till you walk with me, you are also with you, you are also close, in those moments it is not a matter. My heart is eager to tell you, but there is probably no shortage of desires in your needs.

-Morgan Malla

QUOTES:-

Freedom of speech is a tool for protection, don't use it to attack on others.

-Pardeep Kumar Bogra

Healthy discussion will definitely lead to the solution, arguments can be done forever.

-Pardeep Kumar Bogra

Love is freedom not binding. Powerful are those who likes other's freedom, interference in freedom is weakness.

-Pardeep Kumar Bogra

TALES:-

I miss you…

Each and every second of my life.

And you are the reason of my smile.

Because you're mine and mine.

-Piyush Goyal

Our morning start from love

Our night start from fight

Our night ends with love

And we are still together

Because we are brother & sister

And our relation is pure of love…

-Piyush Goyal

See me sad

She cries herself,

See my happiness

She smiles herself,

Then only my sister

Called my second mother…

-Piyush Goyal

REVENGE

I am love to be amorphous, without hesitation like a song mellifluous. I love to eat and taste the different dishes I cannot resist if to eat I have any wishes.

It's obviously my choice that's why I raise my voice. Doesn't matter if I am not ingenu I loved my father like ingenu. I don't want the iridescent to love I need the person as I am as can love. I am halcyon for my weight I am lilt though my heavy weight.

-Pooja Raval

SONOROUS SOUND OF MY HEART

It sounds mellifluous when you are with me,

The melodious music can create by bee.

The most sweet smell is of petrichor

And to be with you on the seashore

The most difficult hiraeth is to go away

For a minute miss you when you say

This is the most beautiful epoch of my life,

When I was shared all the one or other moment as your wife…

-Pooja Raval

LIFE'S PUZZLE

This is unusual,

Yes, this is unusual,

Two soul meet as casual,

Their bond slowly bloomed to special,

Though they appear two individuals,

Their heart beeps mutual,

They share,

They care,

They flare,

Endlessly with no reluctamce,

With acceptance,

To respect each other,

They now bothered not for cracks,

They now bother not for the hail storm,

They are sure of this speciality,

Keeping no complexity,

Rather,

Freedom to groom this special bond with opportunity..

-Prashant Chourasiya

GOLDEN HEART

Wearing my heart on my sleeve,

Blinded by love,

I threw myself at it,

And as I did.

I continued to try to build my home,

I her heart

In a heart that I would later come,

To understand

That it was not ready,

To love someone like me,

With the same depth of love,

I craved in return,

I continued to give all of my love,

Until I poured myself empty.

-Ramshivam Tiwari

TALES:-

I am the sinner and the saint. I am always on time except when I am late. I am courageous except when I am not. I am strong except when I can't leave my house because my soul has been hit by life. I am intelligent and funny and sexy and witty except when I am not. I am stupid and unworthy and not important except when I see my light..

We are all, all of it..

-Ramshivam Tiwari

When I hug you in my thought I feel a crack glass touching my heart but when I hug you in my dreams I feel a magnet is working between us. I know, when I hug you tightly you feel the squeeze of it.

-Ramshivam Tiwari

TALES:-

Evenings with grandma used to be superb when I was young, she sings and my little sister & I use to dance. At night going to the roof with her and counting the stars was one of the most memorable time I could never forget. Although I know no one can count the countless stars in the sky but I enjoyed it. After harvesting crops making small huts of the huff at the roof and playing inside it with dinner and sweets was a great fun. Then at the end sleeping at the roof with family was the most loving experience. But now as the time passes I'm not getting that much time to spend with my grandma. That nights are same but the loneliness feeling makes it different. Ah! I wish that time could come when I was a small child.

-Riya Chaudhary

Past is not a thinking it's an emotion. An emotion that remains with you forever whether good or bad you can't deny good memory will give you refreshment. Bad memories will make you realize your mistake and not to repeat that mistake can lead you to the path of success.

-Riya Chaudhary

Life isn't always easy nor complicated. The reality is that how you see the problem? How you face the challenges in life? how you think about a matter? The problem only arises when we think so much but we just need to keep calm and chill and shouldn't think so much and the problem would be solved definitely.

-Riya Chaudhary

QUOTES:

Bring your way to the brighter, brighter makes you better, better gives you greater, greater provides you pride.

-Sai Prasanna Goud

Your success is what fires your past and light up your future but it burns your present.

-Sai Prasanna Goud

No one can make your life better until the real one wakes from you.

-Sai Prasanna Goud

LOST

Lost I am in a whirlpool of secrets,

Struggling hard even to recognize myself,

My soul now seems to be a stranger to my mind,

My senses turned numb, gullible and blind,

Digging deeper everyday into this darkness of ignorance,

Despite my suffocated, claustrophobic breaths,

Feeling like the oxygen is now rusting my lungs,

My insight turned indifferent and my inside turned dumb.

I keep wandering through pathless, untrodden roads,

Even on knowing that I am headed all wrong,

But I can't help myself from staggering astray.

My strides being too fond of defying the compass needle.

Thus I allow my well acquainted self,

Get fully swallowed by this bizarreness,

As my heart starts beating on an unknown note,

Hearing the only doorway out bring slammed close..

-Sanchari Mukherjee

'S' DIFFERENCE

Smartness and Shyness both start with 'S',

So does 'Selfish' and 'Selflessness'

'Surprise and 'Shock' so led by 'S'

'Sweetness' and 'Soury' have their own ways.

'Satisfaction', 'Sadness have the similar lead,

'Sanity', 'Sneakiness' following the same head

'Science', 'Spirituality stalking the aforesaid rule

'Strength', 'Short-coming' beginning with same tool.

-Sanchari Mukherjee

"TRIBUTE TO MOTHER"

My mother's heart is so tender

And her face has a gentle glow

She is my friend and my inspiration,

She is the sweetest mom I know..

She gives herself so freely

To those who share her life,

She clearly loves her children

With the love that comes from Christ…

Her eyes are full of compassion

Her voice is soft and mild

She lives for helping others,

Leaving "heartprints" all the while.

My mother's love is special

And grows sweeter with every year

God blessed me with an angel,

She is precious mother, dear…

My Dear mom, I said a prayer for you..

To thank the Lord above

For blessing me lifetime

With your tender-hearted love..

I thanked God for the care

You have shown me through the years,

For the closeness we have enjoyed

In time of laughter and of tears..

And so, I thank you from the heart for all you have done for me..

And I bless the lord for giving me the best mother there could be..

-Sanjay Singh Kirtuniya

THE LIFE

Happy Days of Life Revealed,

Again, it's harshness are peeled,

Precious, pretty, playable,

Paddy fields are more stable.

Yield a secret under underneath,

Blow the air, wave your breath.

Inside something ready to feed.

Rest trust your to lead.

Thousands test proceeded.

Hundred attempts leaded,

Daily days unplayed till now,

And what are they, don't know!

Your Assays are with pray, true!

Some words are really hard,

Are made up of 'End of Start'

Dream of low ways came

And appear for me, for shame.

Feeling sad and morose, If I am!

You told me never struck in jam.

Over parting foolishness,

Under one's pretty careless;

Shape a world for your own.

Ultimate trials are gonna known.

Face it off, is enough for you.

-Saqlain Saquib

QUOTES:-

What success is??

"you could wait for the success,

But you should never wait for the failure.

Because failures teach you what success is."

-Saqlain Saquib

Surreality of Dreams

Dreams are surreal, yet they are so real,

Evading the vicious reality, we chase them in obscurity

Some say that you must dream, while others ignore it as a whim..

Blaming dreamers; they lack clarity!

And are drifting away into vanity

They want us to fail in our pursuit, claiming victory in this dispute,

Warning us about threats of its ambiguity "back off,

Before it drives you to insanity!"

Surviving in this world is not so easy,

"Dreams are just an excuse to stay dizzy!"

They fill our minds with such negativity,

While asking us to face the harsh reality,

Now devoid of dreams we wander,

Embracing reality we surrender.

We start raising questions on morality,

Snatched of everything we rot in adversity.

Still, at times a voice echoes inside,

In the cavern of heart, where it reside..

Was all that dreaming in futility?

Giving up! Was this your reality?

If dreams are what you believe in life,

Rekindle your spirit, get ready for strife

At times we need to trust our own ability,

As not everyone understands the gravity

Dreams are surreal, yet they are so real.

Fulfilling them with sincerity,

Is the only way out of this surreality.

-Saurabh Kajawe

One thing I do for myself is that I pat my shoulder when I do something good, pull myself up when I'm drowning, learn from criticism and write out my soul as that's liberation for me!

-Saurabh Kajawe

QUOTES:-

I loved you without a second thought.

You left me without a second thought.

If I had thought of this before then I would have never tried to tell you about my love

and so there will be no chance for your thought of leaving me!

Your worst Best Friend..

(It's my fault)

-Shanmukha Sirisha

Do you remember the very first time when we shaked hands from unknown strangers to become known friends and the very last time when we shaked hands from unknown friends to become known strangers.

-Shanmukha Sirisha

Sometimes I except a call back.

But, there will be a message "call you later".

That 'call you later' will remain unchanged until I call back again.

-Shanmukha Sirisha

WHEN NO ONE UNDERSTANDS

"Scars all over the body, Trying not to be scream. Sobbing in the corner, Tears flowing as a stream."

Yes, this happens..

This often happens when you don't have a human diary. Often happens when you're not so good at opening up to someone. This doesn't mean that you're always wrong. This doesn't prove that you're the culprit every time. You don't have to blame yourself for everything always. Let others be blamed too! Love yourself, praise yourself, stand up again, Wipe off the tears and pay a tribute to yourself for enduring such tortures. Now it's the time for the person who've hurt you to be maltreated. After all, your strengths support you and most importantly, you're superior than your weaknesses!

-Shivani Panda

Bucket down your feelings when they're drenched. Pour out the sentiments which were struggling among themselves to come out. Vomit out your thoughts when you're suffocated. Drive out the action when you feel it's the time to perform. Let them speak whatever, we're free spirited and no one has the right to put an end to it.

-Shivani Panda

A GRIM MISTAKE

A tale I enumerate.

The soul cries.

The heart tries.

Not to break further.

The naïve me.

Tried to be as much good as I can be

Still somewhere, sometime, I got nobody to be with me,

Forgiveness is dilemma

Bitterness is truth

To be exact, world is not ruth.

-Shivani Pandey

Everyone is prodigious in their own way, we need to realize that. Nobody is quintessential. Everyone's life is messed up, we need to realize that. Nobody knows what one is suffering through, what circumstances he is facing, we need to realize that. So show reverence, be gallant.

It's good, we need to realize that.

-Shivani Pandey

BONDED FOR LIFE

She cried her way along the stairs.

Tears running down her cheeks.

Her heart shuddering with pain.

She knew the day had come

She knew she was heartbroken

She wanted someone to console her

To tell her everything would get back better

she felt lifeless, sadness setting within her.

Yet, she wished to live and smile like the old self

For that person who would never hurt her.

Someone who made her smile and giggle.

Someone who made her in all her highs and lows.

Someone who knew how to create memories with her.

She ran to her and hugged her with all her life, complaining her plight and lows.

For she knew her sister would never really let her go, no matter what

One smile and hug from her sister was all that she needed to get smiling again.

-Vibha Deshpande

PERIODS

One of the most hushed topics in this society. The talks about this subjects is so compressed that even the female population find it uncomfortable to discourse about it in public places. A rapist can go to temple but a bleeding women cannot....

They are not a bad thing, they are good thing. It's gross, it's healthy.

It's not something to be ashamed conscious about. Sanitary napkins are not a luxury item.

It's not something that limits your activities. Awareness must be instilled in men, not only women. Yes, they bleed!

They bleed every month, every year and they lose, much of their blood and for whom? To bring us, on this earth.

While we point her, on her existence?

Ooops! She has stain on her skirt.

Let's tease her for the red today.

And god knows, what else? But mind you, mind you people out there. Next time, you question her. You directly question yourself. You question your existence. Ask questions, don't assume don't shy away. Be educated, be aware on periods men shouldn't be ashamed to see a women carrying a packet of sanitary napkins. They give a look as if it's a "taboo". We should openly talk about it not to use code language for it.

'That week is your super women week.'

GIRLS NO BLOOD SHOULD HOLD YOU BACK...

-Vijay

MEMORIES

Her dark oceaninc eyes,

Dragged me to some other world,

Not letting to come over,

All it did was made me lost.

The beautiful face of her,

With all those curls she had,

'Angel on earth' in true meaning,

The only reason behind my smile.

Until the day it came so bad,

Turning my world upside down.

Frowning and drowning me to sorrow,

Leaving behind all the scars.

Forgetting to forget those memories,

And still wanting to be there.

Cause deep inside the broken heart,

Always lied a special place for her.

But now, when she's no more with me,

There's only the memories which haunts,

Just like the dead rose kept near to heart,

Reminding days when feelings were all alive.

It's too late now for anything to be done,

Living life without you is of no fun.

No sleep, no hope as she was all my dream,

'Was all my mistake', is what my heart screams.

-Yuvraj Chhetri

OUR CO-AUTHORS

Abhinandan, a writer by passion. Born on 23rd June 1991. He is a Govt official by profession, but when the light within him, switches on his pen, wired to ink, make the words glitter.

IG id- @abhinandan_srivastava

Abu Md Zakaria, He is from Assam. He loves to give his time to write various types of things which are present in our mother Earth.

IG id- @abu_md_zakaria

Adityan Dravid, from Lucknow. His passion is doing coding education. He is doing mechanical engineering. His hobbies are Swimming, Reading novels, writing quotes and making videos.

Ahtesham, he is the final year student of civil engineering. He likes to play badminton, listening music and cooking.

IG id- @3amthoughts001

Aiswarya Bose, born on 20th March 2000. She is from Thrissur, Kerala. Bibliophile and Dreamer would define her better.

IG id- @_the_maleficent

Ankita Saloni, a 20 years old ambivert bibliophile who finds herself a perfect blend of sugar, spice and everything nice. Being an author, writer, poet, theatre artist and programming enthusiast. She loves to explore all dimensions of her interests.

IG id- @saloni_ankita

Annu Goyal, her aim is to become a Doctor. She likes poetry, painting, photography and dancing. She says, "Don't think too much just do what makes you happy."

IG id- @annu_goyal_

Annu Priya, from Delhi. She is a psychology student from Delhi University and for her writing is a way of healing.

IG id- @priya.an.nu

Anshu Kumar Choudhary, currently pursuing Bcom(h) from DU. An IIM aspirant. He wants fame in his life. He loves singing and helping others. He believes in spreading smiles and love.

IG id- @_anshu_choudhary1999

Bhojani Ayesha Asif, from Maharashtra. She is addicted to novels. She loves to read and write. Writing is her way of expression. Pen helps her bleed her feelings.

ID id- @bhojaniayeshaasif

Chandra Ghosh, a 3rd year student of English Hons. under Calcutta University. She loves to write poetry and singing.

IG id- @game_with_words

Deep Roy, from Namsai, Arunachal Pradesh. He is doing B.pharma . His passion is to be a novelist. His aim is to be a drug inspector.

Deepak Ninkileri, Vagabond soul surfer of time & space who makes his living teaching yoga, sometimes he use his words of wisdom like swords to solve puzzles in his head.

IG id- @Sky_Bhairav

Devika Radhakrishnan,

An avid reader and insouciant scribbler. She is pursuing graduation in Physics. She loves to wander in thoughts.

IG id- @devika_1303

Disha Sharma, from Meerut (U.P.). She is pursuing degree in forestry from Dehradun, Uttarakhand. She loves to dance and read novels.

IG id- @_disha_sharma3112

G Bala Gomathi, from Thirunelveli.

She loves to write quotes and hikoo. She says, "Love became possible when one loves own self."

IG id- @gbalaquotes

Harsh Karnwal, from Haridwar. He is an NCC cadet. He loves to write and read novels.

Karthik, not a natural writer but he writes what he has lived which felt like it must be written.

IG id- @writer_hobbyist

Lavi Chaudhry, words would not be capable to define the person he is.

IG id- @lavi_chaudhry

Mahmoda Sultana (Mahi), she wants people to hear her words before she became voiceless, she wants people to hear her undertone before she become to dumb to speak, and she wants people to know her story before it ends. IG id- @today's_thought

Mohamed Asif, writer not by profession but as hobby. He says, "He would rather be hated for who he is than loved for who he is not."

IG id- @yazi_quotes

Mohnish, a human who took 2 decades of story to write, his failures revealing a bliss through the timeline inking the diary. Born Tamil, walked through Telugu to ink in English.

IG id- @moh_nish_99

Morgan Malla, a Gorkhali. He is a self-made artist. He is from Dehradun, Uttarakhand. He loves to dance, acting, sketching, writing etc.

IG id- @magical_ink_official

Pardeep Bogra, a software consultant and a spiritual seeker.

Learning music these days, want to use this skill to transform himself.

IG id- @PardeepBogra

Piyush Goyal, from Haridwar. He has completed his diploma in CE from Graphic Era Hill University, Dehradun. He loves to write.

IG id- @i_am_piyush_goyal

Pooja Trivedi Raval (Smit). She knows about 16 languages. She likes to train people for the same. I love to evolve the ocean of my feelings on paper with the pen.

IG id- @Poojshimadri

Prashant Chourasiya, he is pursuing his bachelor in English hons. from DU. His aim to be an IAS officer.

Ramshivam Tiwari, from Sultanpur, Uttar Pradesh. He is a blogger, speaker and halftime teacher. He is the winner of SUBODH award.

IG id- @ramshivamtiwari

Riya Chaudhary from Kotdwara, Pauri, Garhwal (Uttarakhand). She is 16 years old. Writing is her passion. She loves to travel.

IG id- @criya2003

Sai Prasanna Goud, a simple poet with strong words. He has made his hobby into passion.

IG id- @Sai8_5_0

Sanchari Mukherjee, from West Bengal. She is a student of 11th standard. She loves writing and singing.

Sanjay Singh Kirtuniya, from Pilibhit, Uttar Pradesh. He is a student, a poet and a writer. He loves to write all types of short poems, stories and tales.

IG id- @Sanjay.Singh.Kirtuniya

Saqlain Saquib, principal of Modern National Academy, Asansol (West Bengal). He is also a translator, writer and a poet. He likes to paint and spend time with nature and friends.

IG- @Pure_heartsaquib12

Saurabh Kajawe, he writes because writing gives him a sense of satisfaction and salvation.

IG id- @MyriadPersonas

Shanmukha Sirisha, from Visakhapatnam, Andhra Pradesh. She has a degree in civil engineering. Her passion is writing. She believes that through writing one can put his heart out.

Shivani Panda from Odisha. A student of class 9th. She has a dark perspective of writing and when she writes. She goes round in circles in the flowery imagination of her!

Shivani Pandey, a student of biotechnology whose hobby is to read and write. Her sole purpose is to make her life story commendable. A simple girl who wants to be a published writer.

IG id- @shivani.pandey_

Vibha Deshpande, a pharmacist by profession. She loves reading books and love to write. She loves to write little snippets of anything she finds interesting.

IG id- @scribbledscriptsbyvd

Vijay, he writes to taste his life twice in the moment and it is retrospect.

IG id- @Vj_janjal

Yuvraj Chhetri, (enigma19) started writing for the sake of expressing his thoughts and the things which he felt inside, slowly writing became his hobby.

IG id- @an_enigmatic_feel